THE LEGENDS OF KING ARTHUR
MERLIN, MAGIC AND DRAGONS

Dados Internacionais de Catalogação na Publicação (CIP) de acordo com ISBD

M469d	Mayhew, Tracey
	The death of Merlin / adaptado por Tracey Mayhew. – Jandira : W. Books, 2025.
	96 p. ; 12,8cm x 19,8cm. – (The legends of king Arthur)
	ISBN: 978-65-5294-170-1
	1. Literatura infantojuvenil. 2. Literatura Infantil. 3. Clássicos. 4. Literatura inglesa. 5. Lendas. 6. Folclore. 7. Mágica. 8. Cultura Popular. I. Título. II. Série.

2025-613

CDD 028.5
CDU 82-93

Elaborado por Vagner Rodolfo da Silva - CRB-8/9410
Índice para catálogo sistemático:
1. Literatura infantojuvenil 028.5
2. Literatura infantojuvenil 82-93

The Legends of King Arthur: Merlin, Magic, and Dragons
Text © Sweet Cherry Publishing Limited, 2020
Inside illustrations © Sweet Cherry Publishing Limited, 2020
Cover illustrations © Sweet Cherry Publishing Limited, 2020

Text by Tracey Mayhew
Illustrations by Mike Phillips

© 2025 edition:
Ciranda Cultural Editora e Distribuidora Ltda.

1st edition in 2025
www.cirandacultural.com.br
No part of this publication may be reproduced, stored in a retrieval
system, or transmitted in any form or by any means, electronic,
mechanical, photocopying, recording, or otherwise, without written
permission of the publisher.
This book is a work of fiction. Names, characters, places, and incidents
are either the product of the author's imagination or are used fictitiously,
and any resemblance to actual persons, living or dead, business
establishments, events, or locales is entirely coincidental.

THE LEGENDS OF KING ARTHUR

THE DEATH OF MERLIN

Retold by
Tracey Mayhew

Illustrated by
Mike Phillips

W. Books

Chapter One

Darkness surrounded him. Coldness seeped into his bones. He shivered.

How he came to be there, he didn't know. He couldn't remember anything, no matter how hard he tried. His mind, usually so clear, was foggy.

Drawing on his powers, he tried to summon light. Nothing happened. He frowned and tried again, willing the energy to come, drawing it from the earth …

A spark – gone in an instant – then nothing.

What was happening to him?

Sighing, he rested his head against the jagged rock at his back, ignoring the way it dug into his skin.

That was when he sensed it.

Magic.

He could feel it in the air. Could taste it like the finest wine Camelot had ever served.

Then he heard them: whispered voices.

He searched the darkness, but found only shadows. He couldn't tell where the voices were coming from, only that they seemed everywhere at once, near and far. Then, suddenly, one was right by his ear.

It was a woman's voice.

'Now you are mine,' it said.

Merlin gasped as he was thrown from the vision, his consciousness hurled back into his body. He stumbled and almost fell as he became aware of his surroundings. The sounds and scents of the forest returned. The whispers of the cave were replaced by a leafy rustle. The coldness became the fading warmth of late afternoon.

Merlin reached out and leant heavily against the nearest tree. Visions, like the one he had just experienced, came upon him without warning, but they hadn't shown his own fate until recently.

Lately he saw himself trapped: sometimes frozen in place, sometimes tied to a rock. It was always dark, and he could never see where he was or who was with him. This was the first time he had heard voices.

He finally understood other people's anger: it was hard knowing only parts of your future. As a boy, when he had told King Vortigern of the dragons beneath the lake, and many times since then with different people, Merlin had not understood their frustration. Now, given mere glimpses of his own fate, he understood it perfectly.

Merlin straightened as a rabbit, obviously spooked, shot out from the undergrowth. It leapt over tree roots before disappearing into the deepening shadows on the other side of the path. Evening was drawing in. He had been away from Camelot for long enough. Merlin's basket was already full, with more than enough plants for his needs. But he loved being amongst the trees, surrounded by nature, and tended to

spend longer on these outings than needed.

Merlin took a deep, earthy breath before setting off along the path home. A sound stopped him after only a few steps.

It sounded like a sob.

Following the sound, Merlin came across a woman sitting against an oak tree.

'My lady?'

Merlin's voice was too loud in the near-silence of the forest. The woman's head snapped up, her long blonde hair whipping across her young face. There was fear in her eyes.

'Do not be afraid, my lady,' he murmured, soothingly. 'I am here to help.'

'Who ... who are you?' she whimpered.

Merlin approached slowly and knelt before her. 'My name is Merlin. I am King Arthur's advisor. What happened? Are you hurt?'

The woman nodded. She wiped her tear-stained face with a trembling hand.

'Camelot is not far,' Merlin said. 'Shall we go together?'

'I don't think I can stand.'

Merlin offered his arm. 'Then let me assist you.'

The woman hesitated before reaching out and taking his arm. Merlin helped her to her feet. Then the two set off together towards Camelot.

Chapter Two

By the time they arrived in Camelot, Merlin was almost carrying the woman. Seeing this, King Arthur ordered a litter to be brought and for the woman to be taken to the infirmary.

As Merlin began to follow her, Arthur placed a hand on his arm. 'Wait, Merlin. Tell me what happened. One moment you were going to collect plants, the next you return with a lady.'

'I was on my way back when I heard her crying,' Merlin explained.

'I couldn't leave her, Your Majesty.'

'No, of course not,' Arthur agreed. 'Do you know what's wrong with her?'

Merlin shook his head. 'She's clearly in a lot of pain. But I thought it would be better to bring her here and make her comfortable before we try to find the cause.'

'She is in the best hands,' Arthur smiled. 'I'm sure you will soon discover what ails her.'

Bowing, Merlin took his leave. He hurried into the castle, along the corridor to the spiral staircase that led to the infirmary.

Merlin arrived just as Altha finished checking the lady over. Altha was the mother of six burly boys who were now all serving Camelot as squires. She took no nonsense from her patients, but she was good at recognising sickness and disease.

Altha left the woman to rest on the bed before going to share her findings with Merlin.

'Overall, she is well,' she announced. 'Though she does have terrible bruising to her left knee, and she may have sprained her left wrist. I've put a splint on it, just in case.'

'Did she say what happened to her?'

Altha shook her head. 'No. I think she is too frightened. But whether she is frightened of us or what happened, I cannot say.'

Merlin watched the woman's face relax as she drifted into a peaceful sleep, all traces of pain and fear gone.

'I gave her a sleeping draught,' Altha added.

'Then we will leave her to rest,' said Merlin.

♣

Over the next few days, Merlin visited the young woman often. Each time she was either asleep or refusing to speak. Then one day, Merlin was in the infirmary mixing a draught to help ease the lady's pain when a quiet voice asked him: 'What are you doing?'

At first, Merlin thought he had imagined it. But the question was repeated, louder this time. He turned

with the mortar and pestle in his hands to find the young woman watching him intently. Glancing down at the contents of the bowl, Merlin said, 'I'm mixing some plants that will help ease your pain.'

The woman moved to the edge of her bed and gingerly placed her bare feet on the stone floor. 'What plants are you mixing?'

Merlin smiled. For the first time since he had met her, she seemed interested in, rather than just afraid of, what was going on around her. For the first time, too, Merlin noticed how beautiful she was.

He held out the bowl. 'Meadowsweet and lemon balm,' he explained. 'Meadowsweet will ease your pain. Lemon balm will ease your fears.'

She looked up at him. 'You must think me silly to be so afraid of you when you have helped me so much.'

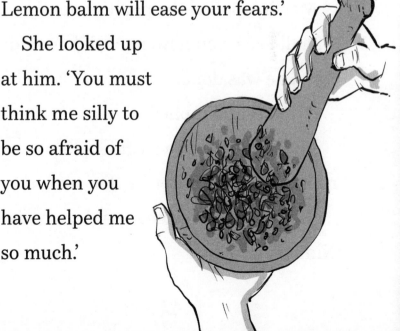

Merlin shook his head. 'Not at all. You have clearly had a fright, and now you are in a strange place amongst strangers. A little caution is natural.'

Merlin finished preparing the poultice. 'Now,' he said, 'I'll just place this on your wrist. It will soon help with the pain.'

'Thank you,' she smiled.

Merlin applied the poultice gently. 'I shall leave you now, my lady,' he said when he was done.

'Nimue,' she replied

The word, spoken so quietly, was nearly missed by Merlin. 'I'm sorry?'

'My name,' the woman said shyly, 'is Nimue.'

Merlin smiled. 'It's nice to finally meet you, Nimue.'

With that, Merlin took his leave, but the smile did not leave his face.

Chapter Three

He had never felt happier. The sun shone down through the trees, dappling the forest path ahead like stars. Birdsong filled the air, but best of all, Nimue walked beside him. He smiled as he watched her. She took such simple pleasure from everything around her: a flower, an insect, a squirrel …

Nimue turned to find him watching her and smiled. It made his heart beat faster. She was looking at him as if he were the only man on earth.

He said something – he scarcely

knew what – but it made her laugh. The sound was more beautiful than anything he had ever heard.

Suddenly, the path before them darkened. A cloud passed overhead and the first few drops of rain fell. Nimue pulled up her hood and ran ahead to look for shelter. Merlin followed. When they stopped and Nimue took down her hood, she looked different. She was *different.*

Her face shifted and twisted before his eyes until it was no longer fair and full of childlike glee, but dark and angry like the growing storm. Reaching into her robes, Nimue pulled out a dagger. Before he could step back, she lunged.

Merlin's eyes snapped open, his heart pounding. Sweat covered his body, chilling his skin. For a moment, he lay in bed, willing his mind and heart to calm.

Another dream, this time about Nimue.

Nimue.

Just the thought of her warmed him, and made the dream seem more ridiculous than worrying.

Nimue was so kind and gentle, she wouldn't hurt anyone!

Merlin dressed quickly and made his way to the infirmary, eager to see Nimue again. The castle was just waking up and servants were going about their early chores before the king and queen rose. Merlin greeted those he passed.

Reaching the infirmary, he found Nimue sitting on the edge of her bed.

She seemed tense and out of sorts.

'Good morning, my lady,' he said. 'Are you well?'

Nimue looked up at him. 'Merlin,' she murmured, smiling faintly. 'I am quite well. It's just …'

'Just what?'

'I feel trapped here,' she confessed. 'I am not used to spending so much time indoors. I need fresh air and the sun on my face.'

Merlin could understand this perfectly: he loved the outdoors and knew from his dreams how terrible it was to be trapped inside.

'Then may I suggest a walk around the castle?' he said. 'Your knee is improving and the exercise will help strengthen it.'

Her smile widened. 'Will you come with me?'

Merlin smiled back. 'I would like nothing more.'

'May I ask you a question?' Merlin asked, eager to end the lengthening silence between them as they reached the courtyard. Despite his many years, it seemed the presence of a pretty lady could still tie his tongue in knots.

'Of course,' Nimue replied.

'What happened the day I found you?' he asked. 'How did you hurt yourself?'

Nimue shrugged. 'I often ride through the woods,' she said lightly. 'That day something scared my horse. She threw me and ran off.'

'It's strange we did not meet there before,' Merlin said thoughtfully. 'I go to the woods often myself.'

'Perhaps it was fate that we met when we did.'

'Perhaps.'

'Now can I ask *you* a question?' Nimue asked, abruptly.

'Of course.'

'Since I've been here, I've heard stories about you,' she began. 'Stories of the power you possess. I think I saw some of that yesterday, didn't I? When you mixed the poultice?'

Merlin looked away. No conversation about his powers had ever ended well. Most of the time, the truth frightened people. 'What you saw was me demonstrating a knowledge of herbs and healing, nothing more,' he answered.

'You and I both know it was more than that,' she insisted. She stopped walking and placed a hand on his arm.

'Merlin, there is no need to pretend with me. There is truth in the stories, isn't there?'

Merlin hesitated, but looking into her eyes, he saw something he had never seen in anyone outside of Camelot: understanding. 'I can see what is to come,' he said. 'Sometimes, I can see a person's fate.'

'Can you see *my* fate?' she asked eagerly.

Not only was she not frightened, Merlin marvelled, she was excited!

'I cannot control it,' he explained. 'Visions come upon me when I least expect them.' Then, seeing her disappointment, he added, 'But I can turn myself and others into animals. And I can control the elements.' He wasn't sure why he was telling her all this. Was he showing off? Certainly Nimue was looking at him very admiringly.

'You can really do all of that?' she breathed.

Merlin took a step back. 'Watch,' he instructed, as he held his hand out. Calling on his power, he felt the heat rise within him, until a small ball of fire floated above his palm. Nimue gasped.

'Wait ...' Merlin murmured, turning his power in on itself. The ball of flame became a bird, its wings flapping above his palm. Then, thrusting his hand skyward, he released it into the air.

Nimue clapped delightedly. 'Show me something else!'

Merlin laughed. 'I think you've had enough excitement for one day.'

'But–'

'Nimue, it's time you rested.'

'I will only go if you promise to show me something else another day!'

Merlin would have done anything she asked, so he nodded. 'As you wish.'

Later that day, Merlin took his seat next to King Arthur in the Great Hall. Arthur turned to him with a knowing look in his eye.

'How is your patient?'

'She is doing well, Your Majesty.'

'I am pleased to hear that,' the king said. 'I saw you in the courtyard with her this morning. You looked happy.' Merlin said nothing. 'There's nothing like the love of a good woman to make a man smile, is there?' As he spoke, Arthur reached for Guinevere's hand.

'I would not know, Your Majesty,' Merlin said.

'Oh, come now, Merlin,' Arthur laughed. 'I've seen the way you look at her. In all the years I've known you, you've never looked at a woman that way. You're in love, whether you want to admit it or not.'

Arthur's words stayed with Merlin, playing over and over in his mind. It was true: Nimue was beautiful and charming, and Merlin had never felt this happy before. But ... was this love?

Chapter Four

A few days later, Merlin entered the infirmary, lost in his thoughts. He was tired from another restless night, and had woken yet again from one of his strange dreams. They came to him every night now, and still he could not tell what they meant.

'Merlin!'

He turned at the sound of Nimue's voice, his spirits lifting as they always did when he saw her. 'Good morning, my lady. How are you today?'

'Bored,' she replied. 'Why haven't you visited me these last few days?'

'King Arthur needed my counsel. But I am here now.'

Nimue's eyes shone with excitement. 'I was wondering if you had forgotten your promise.'

'My promise?'

'To show me more of your powers,' she reminded him. 'You haven't forgotten, have you?'

Merlin shook his head. 'Of course not. What would you like to see?'

At Merlin's command, the water horse reared up, kicking its forelegs before leaping and landing in mid-air above the river. Sunlight reflected off its rippling muscles, creating a rainbow of light as it frolicked. Merlin waved his hand and the water fell back into the river.

'That was beautiful!' Nimue exclaimed. 'When did you discover that you could control fire and water?'

Merlin smiled. 'It was no discovery. It has taken many years of practice.

I studied with the Druids of Avalon. Have you heard of them?' Nimue shook her head. 'Magan, my teacher, took me there as a boy. He taught me all I know.'

'Were you born with these powers?'

Merlin avoided her eyes as he answered. 'My father was a demon.'

'A demon?' she whispered.

Hearing the fear in her voice, Merlin turned to her. '*I* am not a demon, Nimue.'

'But you are a *half*-demon,' she reminded him.

'True, but I have only ever used my powers for good. When I was a child, I had to choose between following the Light or the Dark. I chose the Light. Others with magical abilities did not.' Merlin's thoughts were on one "other" in particular – Arthur's youngest half-sister, Morgan le Fay.

Eager to change the subject, he asked, 'Is there anything else you'd like to see before we return to Camelot?'

Nimue thought for a moment. 'You said that you could turn into an animal – I'd like to see that!'

Merlin nodded. 'As you wish.'

Stepping away from the riverbank, Merlin closed his eyes and thought of an animal. Soon his body began to vibrate with energy. His bones shifted. His spine popped. He was shrinking, coarse red fur sprouting all over his body. Falling to his knees, the bones in his face lengthened

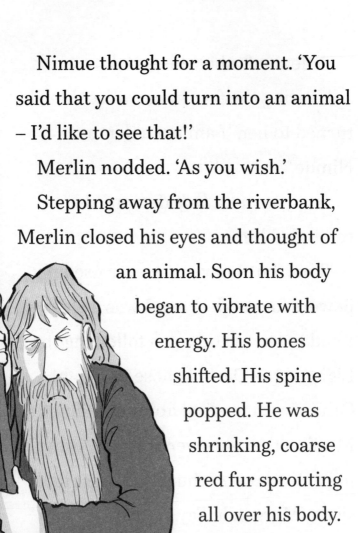

and a muzzle appeared in place of his nose. He shook his head as his ears stretched uncomfortably, his senses heightening with them. Suddenly he could hear for miles. But he could not hear Nimue.

The breeze stirred Merlin's bushy tail as he opened his eyes. Nimue was gone. He sniffed the ground. Her scent was still there, leading off into the trees.

Quickly, Merlin transformed back from a fox into a man. He found Nimue leaning against a tree, sobbing quietly. His stomach clenched at the sound.

'Nimue?'

She jumped at the sound of his voice.

'Nimue, please …' Merlin took another step towards her.

'Don't come any closer!' she cried, backing away. 'You … You were … What did you do?'

'What you asked me to,' he said. 'I should have prepared you for the change. I'm sorry.'

Nimue wiped her eyes. 'You looked so …' She sniffed. 'Did it hurt?'

'It did at first, but no longer.'

'It scared me,' she admitted quietly.

'I'm sorry.'

Nimue smiled shakily. 'And I'm sorry for running away. Perhaps ...'

Merlin watched the uncertainty return to her face. 'Perhaps what?' he asked.

'Perhaps, if I understood your powers better ...'

'What do you mean?'

But she was already shaking her head. 'It's nothing. It's foolish.'

This time when Merlin approached her, Nimue did not shy away. 'Tell me,' he urged her.

'Could you ...' She hesitated. 'Would you teach me what you know?'

It was so unexpected that Merlin almost laughed. But if knowing more about his powers would make her less fearful of him, then he already knew his answer.

Chapter Five

Days turned to weeks and weeks to months as Merlin began his lessons with Nimue. It was clear from the start that she was a very driven and determined student. She listened closely to his instructions, asked questions where necessary, and sometimes even made notes on scraps of parchment. Merlin took pride in the speed of her progress.

Glancing at the pot brewing in the hearth one day, Merlin announced, 'I think we can take it off the heat now.'

Leaping to her feet, Nimue picked up a cloth. After wrapping it several times around the handle, she lifted the iron pot from the hook and moved it onto the worktable.

'Now, can you remember what I told you to do next?' Merlin asked.

'I need to add the ground elecampane,' she recited, reaching for the glass jar containing the ground plant. She consulted her notes before adding the required amount to the pot and mixing it.

Once it had cooled, Merlin announced, 'I think it's ready to take to the patient.'

They left the infirmary, making their way through Camelot and out into the courtyard, towards the stables where their patient waited. Entering the stables, they made their way to Hengroen, one of King Arthur's horses. Hengroen was a huge, majestic stallion, but a few days ago he had developed a skin irritation on his back and was now looking rather forlorn.

Arthur was already in the stable. After greeting Nimue, the king turned to Merlin. 'I think it's getting worse.'

Stepping closer to Hengroen, Merlin inspected the area carefully. He could feel Nimue standing close by, watching his every move. The horse flinched when Merlin touched his back gently.

'The skin is still rough and hot to the touch, Your Majesty,' Merlin said. 'But I do not think it's worse.' Merlin

turned to Nimue and nodded. She immediately began to prepare the poultice. 'This poultice will help. We will apply this three times a day. In a few days Hengroen should be back to his old self.'

Arthur breathed a sigh of relief. 'Thank you, my friend!'

'You seem quiet, Nimue,' Merlin observed on their way back to the infirmary. 'Is everything alright?'

Nimue sighed. 'I'm bored!'

'Bored? With Camelot? With me?' Merlin couldn't hide his disappointment.

'Bored of making potions!' she exclaimed. 'I want to know *more*.'

'What do you mean?'

Nimue turned to him. 'I want to know what you experience when you change into an animal,' she said.

'But I thought it scared you?'

'It did but ... I can't stop thinking about that day. There is a part of me that wants to experience it for myself. Can you understand?'

'I can.'

'Then will you show me?'

As usual, Merlin agreed. 'Come with me,' he said.

♣

The clearing was quiet and secluded.

'I'm scared, Merlin' said Nimue.

'Don't worry,' Merlin reassured her. 'I will make it as painless as possible.'

'Thank you.'

'Now, which animal would you like to become?'

Nimue thought for a moment. 'I've always wanted to fly,' she admitted.

'A bird, then,' Merlin said. 'Close your eyes and relax.' Once Nimue's eyes were closed, Merlin raised his arms and pictured a raven in his mind's eye. He imagined everything, from the creature's black marble eyes to its obsidian feathers.

Nimue began to change, shrinking and erupting in magnificent, iridescent feathers. Her arms twitched and became wings. Finally she released an ear-splitting cry, flapping and hopping in her new form. Merlin watched as

her bird instincts took over and she leapt into the air. She released another cry as she rose higher and higher …

Suddenly, Merlin was beside her, now a raven as well. They flew together, looking down first over the woods and then over Camelot, all the way to the next village and beyond, across fields to the sea and back again. Merlin could feel Nimue's joy as she flew ahead of him, diving steeply before rising at the last moment.

Merlin had angled his wings to join her on the next dive, when a sharp, searing pain pierced his head. He cried out, his vision blurring, his wings forgotten. He fell from the sky like a stone.

Chapter Six

Slowly, Merlin became aware of a frantic squawking. He opened his eyes to find a raven hopping over him where he lay in a field. He had managed to transform himself back into his human form and slow his descent before he landed, but he had forgotten about Nimue.

Sitting up, he whispered a spell.

'You're alive!' she cried happily, back in her own form. 'When I saw you fall I feared the worst. What happened?'

'I don't know.'

But that was a lie.

Merlin knew exactly what had

happened: he'd had another vision. Only this time it had been more detailed, more revealing.

'We must return to Camelot,' he announced, getting to his feet.

'But are you well enough?'

'Perfectly well,' he insisted . 'And I have a matter of great importance to discuss with the king.'

Merlin approached King Arthur's receiving room with a heavy heart. Nimue had begged to accompany him but for once he had refused her: he needed to speak to Arthur alone.

The guards stepped aside, nodding

a greeting as they opened the door. Arthur was inside looking at some papers.

'Your Majesty, may I speak to you?'

'Of course,' Arthur said. 'What's the

matter? You look like you've seen a ghost!'

'Your Majesty, I have grave news,' Merlin said.

'What news?'

'The time has come for me to leave Camelot.'

'What?' Arthur demanded, leaping from his chair. 'You can't leave!'

'I'm afraid I have to. My time here is drawing to a close. I must leave to sleep my long sleep.'

'Sleep your long sleep? What does that mean?'

Merlin had known this would not be easy. 'I will not be returning to Camelot, Your Majesty.'

'But you cannot leave! As your king, I forbid it.'

Merlin smiled. 'As my king, I know you will not stop me.'

'But I need you,' Arthur insisted. Merlin couldn't help remembering the young farm boy he had met so many years ago.

'I wish I could stay, Sire, but I cannot. Fate calls to me.'

'But if you stay, your fate could change,' Arthur reasoned.

'It does not work that way, Your Majesty.'

'Your mind is made up?' When Merlin nodded Arthur sighed and shook his head, looking suddenly weary. 'Then I will miss you, my friend.'

'I will miss you too,' Merlin echoed.

The two embraced warmly. Merlin thought that the king had become a little thinner in recent months. He had been working too hard, and yet Merlin had more to burden him with.

Stepping out of the embrace, he lowered his voice, even though

the doors were closed. 'Be wary of those closest to you, Your Majesty,' he warned. 'Betrayal will come to Camelot if you are not careful.'

Arthur laughed. 'Even now you are still talking in riddles! I tell you, I won't miss that about you.'

'Your Majesty, you *must* heed my words,' Merlin insisted.

Arthur nodded more seriously. 'Of course I will, my friend.' He was silent for a moment before adding, 'I hope you find peace wherever you go.'

'Thank you, Your Majesty.'

Then Merlin bowed for the last time and left the receiving room.

As Merlin led his horse from the stable, he was surprised to find Nimue waiting for him.

'Where are you going?' she demanded.

'I am leaving Camelot.'

'Why?'

'It is hard for me to explain. My fate lies far from here.'

'Then let me come with you.'

'I cannot. Where I am going, I don't know what will happen.'

Nimue began to cry. 'But I don't want to say goodbye.'

'You would do well to stay here,' Merlin said. 'After your efforts with Hengroen, there is no doubt that King Arthur would let you.'

'But I don't *want* to stay here without you!' she insisted. 'I love you!'

Merlin stared at her, unable to believe what he was hearing. Without warning, Nimue kissed him.

'Please take me with you,' she begged.

'Do you understand what leaving with me would mean?' he asked, when he was capable of speech. 'I don't know where I am going or how long I will be without shelter.'

Nimue took his hands in hers. 'It doesn't matter so long as we have each other.' Again, Merlin was struck speechless. Nimue smiled. 'Is that a "yes"?'

Of course it was.

Chapter Seven

Merlin continued teaching Nimue as they travelled. By day she learnt about nature and the power of the earth. At night he taught her how to read the stars. The one thing he never discussed with her were his dreams, but they continued.

'Do you regret leaving Camelot?' Merlin asked her one day.

'Not for a moment.'

'Life there would have been far more comfortable than travelling with me.'

'But without you I would be unhappy,' Nimue replied simply.

It made Merlin feel even guiltier for the knowledge that he would soon be leaving her.

Looking up, Merlin noticed that the evening was drawing in. 'We should find somewhere to rest,' he said.

Nimue nodded eagerly. 'I could certainly use the warmth of a fire. Come, I know somewhere we can shelter.'

Before long she had led him to the mouth of a cave, half hidden by hanging vines and briars. As Nimue dismounted, she noticed a strange look on Merlin's face. 'Are you unwell?' she asked anxiously.

Merlin barely heard her. 'I know this place,' he murmured.

'You do?'

Merlin wandered into the cave like he was in a trance. 'In my dreams ... I am trapped here. There are voices – women's voices ...'

Merlin stopped walking. Suddenly everything made sense.

'It was you,' he said, turning to Nimue.

'I was wondering how long it would take you,' she murmured.

Merlin took a step towards Nimue, towards the mouth of the cave, but she held up her hand. She muttered a spell he did not know that stopped him in his tracks.

'Wanting to learn from me,' he gasped, 'it was all a lie, wasn't it?'

Nimue laughed. It was different from the sweet, playful one he loved. This laugh was cold and mocking. 'I still cannot believe you thought my progress was because of your teachings! I have had another teacher for years.'

A movement at the mouth of the cave drew Merlin's attention. *'You!'*

'We meet again, Merlin,' Morgan le Fay announced. 'It's been far too long.' Merlin raised his hand, but Morgan was careful to keep Nimue between

them as she approached. 'You wouldn't hurt Nimue,' she taunted. 'Not even if it meant killing me.'

Merlin glared at Morgan, hating

himself because even now she was right. He was powerless. 'Nimue, please. Move out of the way. I beg you.'

'I can't, Merlin.'

Morgan's laughter rang out. 'You were so pathetic, Merlin! All those simpering words and lovesick looks! It was all too easy to get the better of you!'

Merlin flinched. It was true. He had fallen for everything Nimue had ever said and now, there he was, alone and at their mercy.

'Is that how Uther tricked my mother?' Morgan demanded. 'Did she fall for *his* declarations of love, too?'

'Uther loved your mother! And despite everything, Igraine loved him, too!'

'Liar!' she spat.

'Believe what you will, Morgan. The truth is that Igraine loved Uther every bit as much as she loved your father.'

Screaming with rage, Morgan had her hands at Merlin's throat in an instant. 'I would kill you myself,' she hissed, 'but I think it would be more

painful if the woman you love had the pleasure. First, you should know that when I am done with you, I will be turning my attention to Camelot and your precious King Arthur!'

Reaching up, Merlin gripped Morgan's wrists. His own rage burst forth as a wall of flame between them.

Laughing, Morgan easily doused the fire, but retreated once more behind Nimue.

'I am bored of this,' Morgan announced. 'Kill him.'

Nimue stepped forwards.

'Nimue,' Merlin pleaded, 'listen to me. It's true, I love you.' Nimue hesitated for a second. 'I know you lied to me, but you are not who she thinks you are. You're a good person. I *know* you are. Morgan isn't to be trusted.'

'What are you waiting for?' Morgan demanded. *'Kill him!'*

Nimue met Merlin's gaze and in that moment, Merlin saw the truth: the woman he loved was still there. He also saw fear in her eyes and knew that she had no choice: she was as much at Morgan's mercy as he was.

Knowing that his death meant that Nimue would live made it easier for Merlin to accept.

Holding her gaze, he repeated, 'I love you.'

Tears filled Nimue's eyes. 'Forgive me,' she whispered.

'I do.'

The earth began to shake and break under Merlin's feet. He cried out in pain as rocks broke free, encasing him from the ground up. He struggled to breathe as the weight of the boulders pressed in on him, rising higher until they surrounded him completely. All the while, Merlin kept his gaze fixed on Nimue, determined that the last thing he saw would be her.

Tears streamed down Nimue's face as she watched the man she loved

disappear from view. She wiped at them angrily, hating Morgan for what she had made her do. 'It is done.'

'I saw the way you looked at him,' Morgan accused her. 'You love him, don't you?'

Nimue glared. 'What does it matter now?'

'It matters because how can I trust you?'

Nimue was silent.

'The simple answer is, I can't,' Morgan continued. 'But I will be generous. Since you love him so much, I will let you stay with him.' With a slash of her hand, Morgan muttered a spell. It turned Nimue

into a hawthorn bush, destined to be by Merlin's side forever.

Then, as promised, Morgan set off for Camelot, and the final stage of her plan.

Continue the quest with the next book in the series!

"This series opens the door to a treasure house of wonderful stories which have previously been available chiefly to older readers. We can only welcome it as a fabulous resource for all who love magical tales, and those who will come to love them."

John Matthews
Author of the Red Dragon Rising series and Arthur of Albion